THE PHANTOM CAT OF THE OPERA

DAVID WOOD ✤ ILLUSTRATED BY PETERS DAY

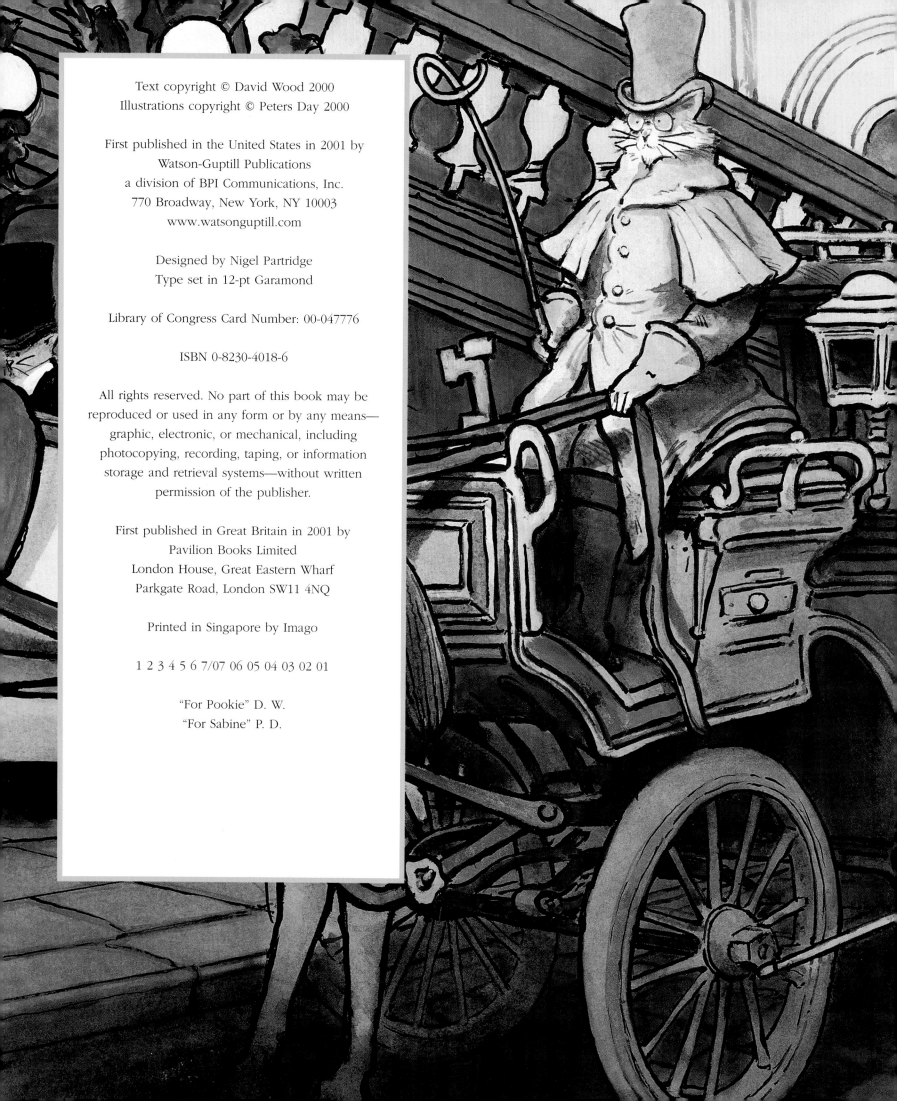

First published in the United States in 2001 by
Watson-Guptill Publications
a division of BPI Communications, Inc.
770 Broadway, New York, NY 10003
www.watsonguptill.com

Designed by Nigel Partridge
Type set in 12-pt Garamond

Library of Congress Card Number: 00-047776

ISBN 0-8230-4018-6

First published in Great Britain in 2001 by
Pavilion Books Limited
London House, Great Eastern Wharf
Parkgate Road, London SW11 4NQ

Printed in Singapore by Imago

1 2 3 4 5 6 7/07 06 05 04 03 02 01

"For Pookie" D. W.
"For Sabine" P. D.

OVERTURE

What was the secret of the Phantom of the Opera? Who was the ghost that stalked the corridors, walked through walls, and terrified all who witnessed his appearances? Did he exist? Or was he really a phantom of the collective imagination, a fantasy figure, belief in whom was fueled by rumor or gossip? For years the well-to-do members of the audience had no inkling of the supernatural occurrences behind the scenes. They came to see the most spectacular productions and hear the most mellifluous music to be witnessed in Paris. For the performances at the Paris Opera exuded unrivaled quality and artistic excellence. And the opera house itself was quite unique in its style and grandeur.

The imposing entrance halls and the grand staircase led to a bewildering maze of halls, foyers, rotundas, and candlelit passageways. And the auditorium was a masterpiece of flamboyant decoration, crowned by a great chandelier. The stage itself was vast and equipped to the highest technical standards. Huge drums underneath winched the scenery up through slots in the stage floor, while sumptuous drapes flew in from high above. Backstage was a warren of wardrobe and property rooms, staircases and corridors, rehearsal studios and dressing rooms, accommodating hundreds of singers, musicians, and dancers; there were even elephants and horses stabled in the cavernous basement and transported to the stage by huge lifts. Below the basement, most magical of all, flowed an underground lake, only discovered when the foundations for the wondrous theater were laid. Could this eerie expanse of water hold the secret of the Phantom of the Opera?

ACT ONE

Much of the mystery was caused by the Phantom's apparent ability to manifest himself in different forms. Young members of the corps de ballet, returning from the stage along dim gaslit corridors, would suddenly see what they could only describe as a living skeleton in full evening dress. "He loomed through the wall," they twittered hysterically. "Under his top hat was a death's head, a skull with black holes for eyes and yellow skin stretched taut over his cheekbones. He brushed past us like a shadow, then disappeared as mysteriously as he'd appeared. Horrible!"

On their regular rounds deep in the cellars, the fire officers would suddenly encounter an advancing ball of fire. "As it came closer," they reported, trembling at the memory, "it became a bodiless, flaming head with staring, haunted eyes, floating through the darkness."

Sometimes the Phantom was invisible. After a performance, his reserved box regularly showed evidence of his presence: the opened program, the half-drawn curtain, the altered angle of the chair. Sometimes a voice could be heard from inside the box. Yet no one ever saw anybody enter or leave. A mystery indeed!

The managers of the Paris Opera decided
to retire. A special gala concert was announced
to celebrate the arrival of their successors.
The specially invited audience members
swept up the grand drive in their carriages.

Carlotta, the renowned resident soprano, was indisposed that night. But Christine, her understudy, sang like an angel. The audience gave her a standing ovation. Raoul, a handsome young aristocrat, had listened entranced from a box above the stage. As Christine acknowledged the rapturous cheers, Raoul felt in his heart the glow of love.

Raoul was convinced that, when they were both very young, he and Christine had met on holiday and had become friends. Eager to discover whether his little companion of long ago and today's new operatic star were one and the same, he hurried backstage.

In her dressing room, Christine was surrounded by well-wishers. Raoul pushed through them.

"Mademoiselle," he whispered admiringly.

"Monsieur," replied Christine, appearing confused. "Who are you?"

Raoul smiled. "Years ago, I rescued your scarf from the sea!"

With no flicker of recognition, Christine turned back to her admirers and resumed her conversation. Raoul departed, deflated. But, determined to meet Christine once more, he lurked in the corridor near her dressing room. He waited for over an hour until all her guests had departed, then, trembling, approached her door. He plucked up the courage to knock, but suddenly he heard a voice from inside the dressing room: "Christine, you must love me." To which came Christine's tearful reply: "How can you talk like that when you know I sing only for you? Tonight I gave you my soul."

The other voice softened. "No emperor ever received such a priceless gift. Tonight the angels wept."

Raoul heard no more. But he had heard enough to feel the pangs of jealousy. He waited in the shadows. He needed to see his rival, to put a face to him. At last the door opened and Christine appeared. But, to Raoul's surprise, she was alone. She closed the door and departed.

Raoul waited, but no one else emerged from the dressing room. He crept out of his hiding place, opened the door, and went in, ready to confront his rival. The gas lamp flickered. Raoul gasped. A shadowy figure stood facing him. Raoul froze. The shadowy figure froze. Raoul stepped back. The shadowy figure did likewise. Then Raoul relaxed as he recognized his own reflection in the dressing room mirror. Otherwise the room was quite empty.

ACT TWO

At a splendid farewell party for the retiring managers, the speeches were suddenly interrupted by a shrill voice: "The Opera Ghost! The Opera Ghost!" Everybody looked where the little ballet dancer was pointing. Among a group of dandies stood a skeletal figure with a death's head. The guests blinked and he was gone.

Pandemonium broke out and the managers ushered their successors swiftly away. In the privacy of their office they explained about the presence of a ghost in the opera. The new managers were highly amused by what they assumed was a practical joke. "We are serious," insisted the departing managers, refraining from admitting that the ghost was their main reason for leaving. "He sends us letters demanding money and a reserved box."

"No ghost will get the better of us!" laughed the newcomers.

And indeed, some weeks later, they chose to ignore the mysterious letter they themselves received. Clumsily written in scratchy red ink, it demanded that Christine should sing that very evening and that the Phantom's special box should be made available for him to hear her performance. The new managers decided that Carlotta should perform as advertised and that the box should be offered for sale to the public. But the next day they received an irate visitation from the occupants of the box, who complained that their evening had been ruined by a disembodied voice constantly complaining that the box was his and insulting the singing talents of Carlotta.

This joke, thought the managers, is going too far.

Raoul was thrilled that Christine had responded to his letter and agreed to meet him. As they took a stroll by the banks of the Seine, he declared his love. Christine sighed. "If only I were free to return your love, dear Raoul."

She explained that, in the dressing room, she had recognized Raoul instantly, but was frightened to acknowledge him. "My angel of music would have been sorely displeased."

"Your angel of music?" asked Raoul gently. "I don't understand. Who is this angel?"

"He inspires me and influences my career," Christine replied. "My dear father, before he died, promised me that I should one day have my own angel. His promise has come true."

She explained that she never saw her angel, only heard his mesmerizing voice—the voice Raoul had overheard from outside the dressing room, the voice that demanded Christine's eternal devotion.

Raoul held Christine tight. They kissed. They knew they were in love. But Raoul had the uncomfortable sensation that, even now, Christine and he were not truly alone.

It was not long before the managers received another threatening letter.

My Dear Managers,

Is it to be war between us?
If you still care for peace:
   1. Give me back my private box.
   2. Christine must sing tonight. Carlotta must be ill.
If you refuse, my curse upon your House.

P.C.

"We must not give in to such nonsensical demands," agreed the managers angrily. "Carlotta will sing."

As for the Phantom's private box, they decided that they themselves would occupy it that night to witness Carlotta's customary triumph. "Let us confront this so-called phantom and settle the business once and for all."

A full house greeted the performance with enthusiasm. The intermission arrived. In their box the managers smiled smugly. So far no sign of the Phantom or his threatened curse. But Carlotta was not due to enter until the next act.

When her moment arrived, her admirers gave her a rapturous welcome. Her music played. She drew a deep breath. She opened her mouth to sing. "Qu-oak." And again, "Qu-oak." An excruciatingly ugly sound, a cross between the quack of a duck and the croak of a toad, echoed through the acoustically perfect auditorium. The audience gasped. The orchestra stopped playing. "Qu-oak," again. The managers tensed. They glanced at each other in alarm. "Qu-oak." Then fear filled their hearts as they felt a tangible presence beside them in the box. A voice began to chuckle. Carlotta, confused and embarrassed, looked at the audience, appealing for sympathy. But the laughter from the box spread rapidly until the whole house rocked in tumultuous uproar.

The managers were appalled and terrified. The voice alongside them stopped its infectious chuckling. "Tonight," it whispered in their ears, "Carlotta is really bringing the house down! See the chandelier!" The managers looked up aghast as the immense mass of the chandelier plunged down from the ceiling. It smashed into the center of the stalls amid cries of wild terror.

Act Three

C hristine, who had been singing in the chorus when the chandelier fell, stumbled in a state of shock to her dressing room. Suddenly she heard the voice of her angel singing as though to calm her. And then she saw him. For the first time ever, her angel appeared to her. His hideous face made her start.

"Don't be afraid, Christine," said the familiar gentle voice. "You are in no danger."

In a trance she allowed herself to be led by him to the mirror, which revolved to let them through. They descended a candlelit staircase to the darkest depths of the opera house.

They reached the underground lake, where a boat was waiting. Christine's angel took the oars and, with a powerful stroke, rowed her across the noiseless water toward his lair.

Christine found herself sitting in an ornate music room. Tears filled her eyes as she realized the truth. Her voice, her inspiration, was here, prostrate before her.

"It is true," said the voice. "I am not an angel. I am not a ghost. I am Erik." He lowered his cruelly disfigured face and tenderly kissed Christine's forehead. She felt repulsion, but was powerless to resist.

"I love you, Christine. I want you to sing for me alone. Forever."

ACT FOUR

Raoul was overjoyed to receive a letter from Christine. Her disappearance had devastated him. Concerned for her safety, yet powerless to protect her, he'd despaired of ever seeing her again. But now she had summoned him to a secret meeting at the opera's annual masked ball.

Escaping the masked revelers on the marble staircase, he pressed through a mad whirl of dancers and waited by the appointed pillar. Suddenly a masked figure in a dark cloak passed by and nudged him meaningfully. Raoul followed Christine away from the brightly-colored assembly, through dimly lit passages to a winding staircase leading to the roof.

They scarcely noticed the breathless sight of Paris twinkling by night beneath them. They removed their masks and kissed. For a lingering moment, their problems melted into the night sky. But then Christine told Raoul everything. How her angel had carried her off. How he was really Erik, a tragic, unfulfilled musician of genius, spurned by the opera management years before and condemned to a secret life of resentment and revenge. Erik, the Phantom Cat of the Opera.

"I love you!" Raoul's voice echoed over the rooftops. "Christine, say you love me!"

"I do, I do," cried Christine, "but Erik loves me too. He wants me to sing for him alone. He still has power over me. I will never be free from my angel of music!"

"Let me remove you from his power," begged Raoul. "Escape with me tonight!"

"I can't," sobbed Christine. "I promised Erik I would return to him tonight."

"What? To his underground prison?"

She nodded. "He only set me free so I could say goodbye to you."

Raoul could not let Christine go. He persuaded her to elope with him immediately after the following night's performance. She agreed not to return to her dressing room after the final curtain, but to hasten to a carriage awaiting her outside. But Raoul had failed to include Erik in his plan. Perhaps he should have foreseen that the Phantom was not finished yet.

Next evening, the concert began. Raoul was watching from his box. Christine was singing. Suddenly the stage was plunged into darkness. There was hardly time for the audience to panic before the gas lamps revived and flooded the stage with light again. But, to Raoul's horror, Christine had disappeared.

Raoul frantically dashed outside. The carriage was still waiting, but Christine was nowhere to be seen. Where was she? Raoul broke out in a cold sweat as he realized the ghastly truth. Erik! This was Erik's work. He must have somehow discovered their escape plan and, mad with jealousy, plotted Christine's kidnap.

Raoul ran back into the opera house and hurried backstage. Pushing blindly past startled stagehands and members of the chorus, he reached Christine's dressing room. The door was open. The room was empty. Recalling Christine's description of her descent to the underground lake, Raoul approached the mirror. He pushed against it and suddenly it revolved to admit him.

His eyes gradually adjusted to the darkness as he stumbled down and down until he found himself in a pitch black passageway. Feeling his way along the damp walls, Raoul suddenly became aware of a strange scuffling, scratching sound. When he looked up he saw a sight that froze him to the spot: a ball of fire, at head height, was floating along the passage toward him. As it came closer, he could distinguish a face within the flames, then two eyes staring straight at him. Raoul felt his hair stand on end with horror. He screamed. Then the head of fire, still advancing, cried out: "Don't move! Don't move! I am the rat-catcher. Let me pass with my rats!" And the head of fire floated past, disappearing into the darkness, followed by the scuffling and scrabbling of a dozen rats. To avoid scaring him, the rat-catcher had turned his lantern upon his face, but now, to hasten the rats' flight, he shone it down the passage ahead.

Raoul breathed again. Once more, he crept along the corridor until he reached the lake. No boat awaited him. Only an uninviting expanse of inky-blue, ice-cold water. Recklessly he jumped in and swam wildly toward a hazy glow of light in the far distance.

As he approached the shore, Raoul could hear the sound of music echoing across the water. An organ thundered, accompanying a magical soprano voice singing a haunting refrain.

"Erik!" shouted Raoul. "Christine!"

The music stopped abruptly and captor and captive appeared on the balcony.

"It is I, Raoul. I have come for Christine."

Erik spoke, soft yet defiant. "Christine is mine. She sings for me alone. I will make her happy."

"If you cage a nightingale," said Raoul, "she will soon lose her song. Set her free. She loves me. And I love her."

Erik turned to Christine. "Is this true?" he whispered.

Christine nodded. Tears welled in her imploring eyes. "You are still my angel of music. You always will be. But, please, I cannot love you."

Erik slowly turned and shuffled inside.

Love unrequited knows no reward. For the sake of Christine's happiness, Erik sacrificed his will to live. And now, with the bittersweet memory of her song ringing deep in his soul, he simply faded away.

Great was the rejoicing at the opera house when Christine returned. She soon became a major star, her singing more beautiful than ever. And it was not long before she and Raoul vowed to live happily ever after. Their happiness was total. Yet when the wedding ceremony was over and Christine sang to entertain the guests, they both sensed the presence of one who had not received an invitation. Unthreatening now, but still with the power to inspire, would the ghost of Erik haunt them forever?

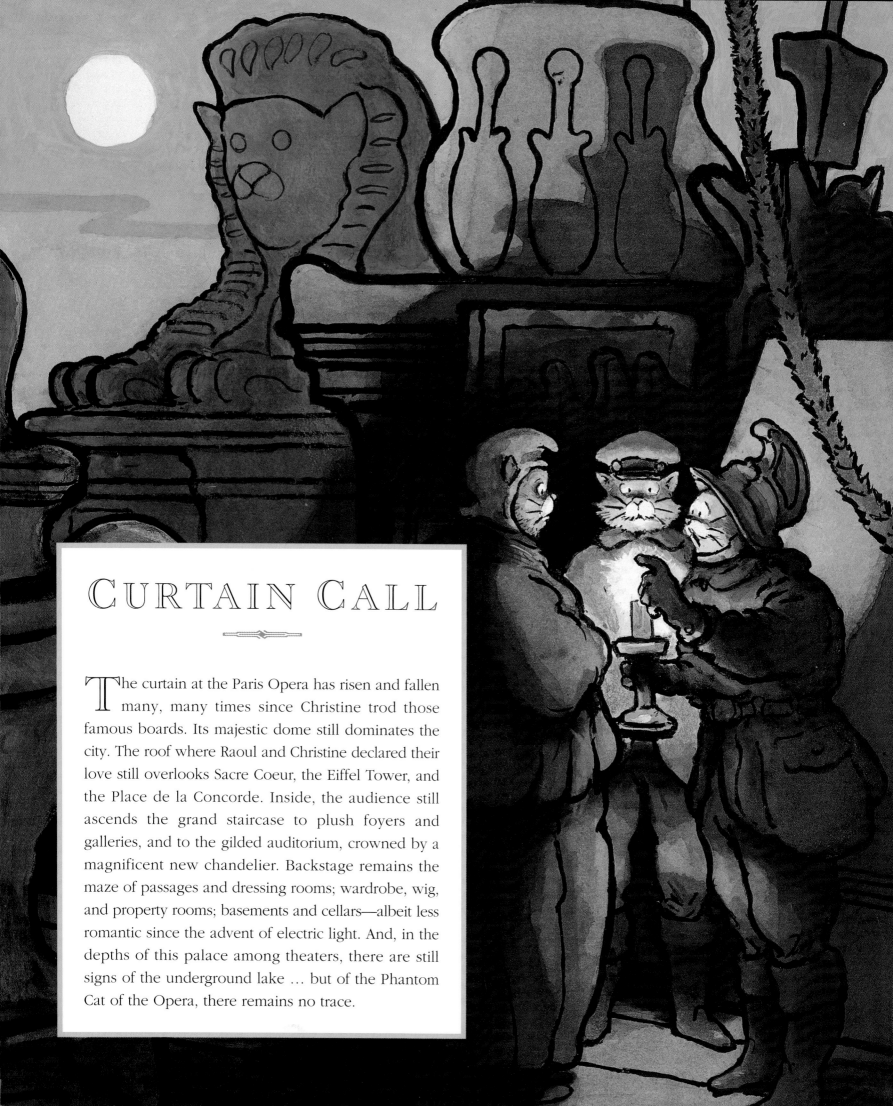

CURTAIN CALL

The curtain at the Paris Opera has risen and fallen many, many times since Christine trod those famous boards. Its majestic dome still dominates the city. The roof where Raoul and Christine declared their love still overlooks Sacre Coeur, the Eiffel Tower, and the Place de la Concorde. Inside, the audience still ascends the grand staircase to plush foyers and galleries, and to the gilded auditorium, crowned by a magnificent new chandelier. Backstage remains the maze of passages and dressing rooms; wardrobe, wig, and property rooms; basements and cellars—albeit less romantic since the advent of electric light. And, in the depths of this palace among theaters, there are still signs of the underground lake … but of the Phantom Cat of the Opera, there remains no trace.